PROLOGUE

TONY HERNANDEZ

THE WHITE CAN

Chapter 1

THEY WERE ONLY A FEW MILES out from their current objective, Talil, a small town on the way to their real target of Baghdad. Ever the overprepared force, the U.S. Army had planned for a long, slow fight. Instead they were moving fast, almost too fast, to bring down Saddam. It was starting to become a logistical nightmare without enough food, water, or supplies as the men marched to their objective. The fighting was small and the pace was fast, leaving most of the men wishing they could trade their bullets for meals.

Staff Sergeant Juan Bocanegra, or Boca as some of his men called him, was of average size—by Iraqi standards, anyway. Back home in Phoenix, he'd been considered short. His Mexican parents had brought him to the United States when he was just seven months old. He'd moved around since he was a kid, so in that respect, being at war was no different.

Most of the troops were comfortable as part of an invading force, but not Boca. He had never felt at home anywhere. Whenever he visited Mexico, the country and culture felt as foreign and distant to him as if he were walking on another planet. And back in Arizona, he was treated and looked at differently because of the color of his skin. He was a stranger even on his own turf, wherever that was.

He'd enlisted in a relatively peaceful time. The World Trade Center still stood, and terrorism was something that only happened to other people on the other side of the TV screen. Joining the military was a path to adventure and a way to pay for college. He chose the Marines—the best of the best. Boca wanted to see if he could stack up, even though at first, he wasn't too sure he would even qualify.

Justin Grant, Boca's newfound friend, had never doubted it. They were both two years in the Corps when September 11th happened.

Originally from Montana, Grant wasn't the smartest guy on the fire team, but that hardly mattered. He had guts, and while he had a bit of a wild streak, he followed orders, and in today's Corps, that was more valuable than gold. Although they were from different worlds, Boca and Grant hit it off immediately, their differences being part of what brought them together. During the buildup to war, Boca and Grant had met Stateside and been put into the same battalion. Constant close contact made time stretch on, and the three months they spent together felt like three years. They enjoyed each other's unique quirks and customs, and physically, they were mirror opposites. Boca had tan skin, brown eyes, and black hair. Grant was blond-haired with blue eyes, and skin that had changed to a shade of pink since the invasion. Boca was short and more stocky in nature, whereas Grant was tall and a bit on the lanky side.

But even though they were as different as could be on the surface, they shared the same soul. They upheld the same values, the same sense of right and wrong. They both happened to come from poor backgrounds, but with parents so proud, you would never have guessed it by meeting them. Secretly they both always wanted to be near one another, as though each was the other's security blanket.

It turned out war wasn't like the movies. There was no taking the hill or hand-to-hand combat. It was one long waiting game, all sitting around and doing nothing. War was a government operation, after all, and governments were best at killing and doing nothing—hence why they excelled at war.

The vehicles they rode in weren't really moving so much as starting and stopping, over and over again. They had to make sure they weren't driving over landmines. A vehicle at the vanguard, called a MICLIC, would shoot an explosive line about a hundred yards. The line would then blow, creating a safe route to travel on. The convoy would move up a hundred yards, stop, prepare another line, then shoot. The process repeated ad nauseam.

At times, the U.S. Army moved into battle with all the speed and stealth of an elderly elephant. It was slow, but it was safe. In theory, at least. While the obvious drawback of going in guns blazing was having all your men get blown up by landmines, it offered the advantages of speed and surprise. On the other hand, entering cautiously—like they were now —gave the enemy more time to prepare for the oncoming attack. It was a no-win situation either way. By the time many of the men got to one of their objectives, some were exhausted from the waiting alone.

But eventually they made it to the outskirts of Talil. It was a fortified village, with walls that weren't too high, but weren't exactly scalable either.

"Five mikes!" the radios said as they came to life, signaling that they would be moving in five minutes.

The order was repeated several times. As they waited inside their armored transport vehicle, an M1 Abrams tank easily pushed open a blue metal gate with its turret.

This is it, Boca thought.

As soon as the rear hatch opened, they were ready for a fight. It was facing away from the village, so the chance they would be shot at as soon as they got off was small. But there was still a chance. Boca thought the inside of the transport was bright, but he was quickly corrected when the hatch opened. The Iraqi sun seemed ten times brighter than back home. At least the air was clean.

As the first squadron poured in and took their positions inside the town, a strange sight welcomed them. Townsmen stood in the street, or looked down at them from buildings. They weren't fighting; they weren't even running. They just stood and stared, as if some strange creature from another planet were parading by.

"Yalla! Yalla!" the soldiers shouted at the people of the town. It was Arabic for *get going*, and the townsfolk complied. It seemed none of them were armed. This was not the big battle Boca had expected.

IT TOOK about an hour to get all the townsmen slowly herded into what seemed to be the town square. No one was totally sure what the place was, but it was the only clean, open air area. Other than this spot, the town was a labyrinth of homes built more on top of each other than next to each other.

The Iraqi men were all flex-cuffed behind their arms and made to sit down against a wall on one side, while the uncuffed women and children were placed across the square from the older men. By the tone of their words, some of the men were clearly fathers to some of the children.

The battalion continued to clear the town, without any fighting. As they went from house to house, it became clear that Saddam's Republican Guard had left. The only people who greeted the soldiers were men cowering in their homes.

After about two hours of kicking in doors and clearing houses, some of the men started growing comfortable. Then they heard gunfire in the distance—the unmistakable sound of an M16. Every available soldier ran toward the sound in support.

Grant got there first and gave Boca a smile when he arrived. They soon realized their alarm had been for nothing. While one of the soldiers was clearing a house, part of a wall had come down behind him. In a panic, he started firing into the area. It was the only battle waged on this day of siege on a new front: a fight with falling stucco.

Chapter 2

F INALLY, AFTER ROUNDING EVERYONE UP, they began the process of debriefing the town. Contrary to earlier reports that women and children were fleeing for safety, it soon became clear that more than a few wives had actually stayed back, even as the fighting was coming to them. Boca wondered how any man could leave his wife in a war zone, knowing full well she might die. It spoke more to her character than his.

Through their terp—as the Iraqi translators were known—they found out everything they were going to find out. In a word: nothing. Everyone in the village stuck to the same version of the same story.

They were all just poor townsfolk.

The men who had fled the night before? They had no idea who they were.

No one could even remember their faces.

If you asked Boca, it was a convenient time for mass amnesia.

Slowly, as day became night, they allowed the men to return to their wives and children, and go back to their homes. The pushback was nearly instantaneous. When one of the sergeants asked for a list of the abandoned houses from one of the townsmen, he was told that every building was occupied, even though it was a near ghost town and there were more buildings than people. The sergeant then asked if there was any running water or restrooms; the man claimed all their toilets and faucets were broken.

Since the town wasn't going to be cooperative, platoon leader Lieutenant Eric James Day ordered the patrols to begin watch over the town. Lieutenant Day was a good and straightforward leader, a by-the-book kind of guy. He tried to be as easy as he could with his men, but when it was time to work, it was time to work.

Lieutenant Day was just under six feet tall. His height didn't provide him with a naturally commanding presence, but when he entered a room, men stopped whatever they were doing and came to attention. He had clear blue eyes as intense as the pulsing muscles in his jaw. His blond hair was cut close, adding to the Boy Scout image he gave off. In fact he had been a Boy Scout, and at just twenty years of age, Lieutenant Day was in charge of men older than he. It was the youth leading the youth into battle, their commanders trusting their training to speak for them in battle.

Night had fallen on the town. Boca and his squad took the western part, knocking on doors they had cleared earlier. It was obvious which houses had people in them. Earlier in the morning, all the houses had been cleared, and all the doors no one answered had been kicked in. Those that remained broken were empty, while those that had their doors up, no matter how battered, were the ones with people inside.

The team stopped when they saw a group of men inside a small alley. They soon found themselves in a short staring contest. The stares ended, and the Iraqi men continued on talking and smoking cigarettes. Boca could've used a cigarette right about then, too. He got on his radio. "Sir, we found a few empty houses down here with running water. Toilets, showers." Boca gave their coordinates.

"Copy that. We'll bring a second group there shortly."

"Roger, out."

As Boca and his men waited, he looked at the group of Iraqis. Most of them seemed to be focusing their attention on one member of the group in particular; in fact, they had formed a horseshoe around him. He had on some type of Iraqi sweater vest. Boca never understood that. *All this heat and dudes are rockin' sweater vests?* The sandbox became more of a mystery to him every day.

Sweater Vest nodded his head to some things the other men said, and shook his head at others. They were all whispering, though Boca wasn't sure why. Boca's men were half a group away, and besides, they were nothing more than a group of monolingual Americans, for the most part. The Iraqis could be talking about how they were going to cut Boca's throat right in front of him, and neither he nor his men would have understood a word.

Then the kids started to arrive. At first they gathered around the Iraqis. Eventually, one of the kids, who was wearing a traditional long shirt that looked like a dress, kept glancing over at Boca's men. He stood there, one hand in his mouth, gnawing his fingernails, while the other arm rested on his hip. To most Americans, this might look like a feminine gesture, but to Iraqi men and boys, it was a common mannerism.

One by one, the Iraqi men left for the evening. One by one, the coalition forces relieved each other for a dry shower and a much-needed break. The only one to leave with a menacing stare toward the Marines was Sweater Vest.

Only once he was gone did Boca dare take his break.

THE NEXT MORNING there was an impromptu town meeting. The entire village, or what was left of it, showed up to the town center. They weren't there to listen as much as complain, and to ask for money and help. According to each one, coalition forces had destroyed their houses and livestock.

Lieutenant Day wasn't even sure whether these buildings had already been destroyed before Operation Iraqi Freedom or not, and he could not for the life of him figure out how all the cows had been vaporized, because there was no sign of them or their corpses. These men were clearly trying to milk him. And to some extent, he'd let them. He was part of an occupying force. He also knew that one of the best moves was to get those against you on your side as soon as possible. History showed there was no better method for doing that than money. As soon as he found a window to escape all the requests he couldn't understand, he climbed on top of an Abrams tank.

The masked terp joined him atop the tank and the lieutenant began to address the small, but growing, crowd.

"We are not here as conquerors, but as liberators," Day said. The response was unchanging stares. "We want your village and your lives to go back to normal as soon as possible. Hopefully, life for you will be better here in a few years because we came here." The only noise other than Day's voice was the wind. The entire village was looking at him. Meanwhile, all the armed forces were looking at the villagers, waiting for one of them to do something stupid.

A man began to bark at Lieutenant Day, lifting his hand up and down. The translator tried his best to speak as fast as he could.

"He says you've destroyed his village. You've killed his men."

"Please," Day began to plead, "tell him we are not

here to harm him or his family. Our fight is with Saddam."

The village started to talk among themselves after that. Maybe bringing up Saddam's name hadn't been the best idea. This was a Sunni Muslim town, after all, and the Sunnis were loyalists to the Saddam regime.

Boca was about twenty yards away from Day's makeshift soapbox and could hear Day clearly, but his attention was on the villagers. The man who was giving the lieutenant lip was none other than Sweater Vest. He'd referred to the men in the village as *his* men, which meant he was definitely the big dog in town.

"In the meantime, we will have to use your town as a staging point for our operations. Again, we want to be in and out of here as soon as possible. Hopefully, we can all work together." With that, Lieutenant Eric Day and his interpreter hopped off the tank. As the villagers began to crowd Day again, Boca made a beeline to him first.

"Sir." Boca tried to talk over the crowd. "I know who the town sheik is."

"Who is he?"

"There." He pointed to the mustached man, who

still had on the same sweater vest from the previous night. He was smoking a cigarette.

"Loud mouth? Fine, get him over to HQ. I need to have a chat with him."

THE SHEIK WAS ESCORTED into the tent that served as makeshift headquarters. In Iraq, the sheiks were the town's leaders, and this one was not very happy with what he saw. Just a little over twenty-four hours in, and the Americans had already made his village into their home. The communications and elaborate setup were intimidating, even if it hadn't been their plan. The Americans were fast conquerors.

Sheik Mufaddal Jabr Bousaid was thirty-five years old but looked more like he was pushing fifty. The grey in his roots rebelled against the bad hair dye he applied to his hair and mustache. The deep lines in his face didn't help him look any younger.

His eyes were as deep and dark as ashtrays, and he had the smell to match. He looked like he was constantly upset, as if he had an eternal splinter and no plans to get rid of it. He was content with his misery.

His young age afforded him well-deserved respect among the Americans. Most village elders were, well, elderly. Not this one. There were other men in the village who were much older than him, but they listened to his command nonetheless. How he had become sheik was anyone's guess. More than likely, it was by spilling blood for his master Saddam.

Sheik Bousaid made himself at home and began talking to the interpreter. "We have done nothing, yet you come here and attack us! You destroy the village and our way of life! How are we ever going to be able to profit again?"

Day kindly nodded as the man aired his grievances. Basically, everything he was upset about was the Americans' fault. Day listened, hoping this man would burn himself out soon. After about five minutes into his diatribe, he lifted his hands up in frustration and stopped speaking.

"I understand that you're no fan of ours. I get that. Be we ain't leaving." Day glanced over to make sure the masked interpreter was relaying his message with the appropriate directness. "You want us out. We want to *be* out. The sooner you and your village begin cooperating with us, the sooner we can leave."

"What can we do? How can we cooperate? We

have nothing. Everything has been blown away by your bullets," Bousaid said.

"What we need is information, and no interference. That means you start telling us what you know and you don't harm us in the process."

"I've already told you everything."

The back-and-forth went on for nearly an hour. Every chance the sheik had to take a dig at the Americans, he took. Not that the lieutenant could blame him. The mortar fire had put some nice holes into the town. Also, this was a Saddam village. They were part of the bad-guy team. Bad guys generally didn't like the good guys.

When everyone in the room was mentally exhausted, they let Bousaid go back to his village. They hadn't gotten a single new piece of information from him. Apparently, all the armed men who had made their homes here for a few weeks were unmemorable.

Frustration was at least better than death. Though what worried Day the most was the quiet. His men seemed to feel safe; they were being lulled into a sense of security. There was no visible threat. There was a sort of peace.

It was only a matter of time before that peace would be broken. Of that, Day was certain.

THAT VERY DAY, people started returning. Namely women and children, but some men, too. Mostly the elderly and disabled. They slowly started appearing on the horizon, and walked steadily toward the town.

How did they know it was okay for them to come back? Bocanegra wondered. That was another strange thing about the Iraqis: They were like birds. They scattered when they felt danger and came back when they knew it was safe again. How they did this, no one was really sure. None of them had phones that he could see. Some of the men called it the "Iraqi sixth sense."

The spokesperson for the new families was the sheik's wife, Zahida Lamis Bousaid. Most of the brass didn't trust her. She was, in all likelihood, just another Saddam supporter like her husband. But Boca saw something different in her. When she walked by, her eyes weren't like the others. There was no anger behind them. She carried herself like a kind, caring person. She always had a child in tow and helped watch over all the children, making sure they ate, studied, and went to sleep as soon as the sun set.

It was their second day in, and with the women returning, the town was starting to feel a little bit more normal—or as normal as a town could feel during a war occupation.

The soldiers posted in the town were on watch over the villagers. This accomplished three things. The first was official, while the other two were just fringe benefits.

The first and main reason to watch over the town was to provide security from any possible attack from the village. There was some apprehension in case of the unlikely event they had to protect the villagers from themselves, but so far, this hadn't been the case.

The other two reasons coalition forces provided security were selfish ones. First, it allowed them to share intel on the town. Every village was different in terms of the people and the customs. After a while, one began to see a pattern.

This led to the third reason for being on patrol: It boosted morale. Going into battle, a soldier's body was on high alert. The fight-or-flight response turned all the way up, and anxiety made every minute feel like an hour and every small noise sound like a firecracker.

That alertness, that edge, that *fear*, slowly began

to fade away as the soldiers went on patrol. The state of constant fear became one of fear mixed with a little comfort. The second was definitely preferable.

BACK INSIDE THE COMMAND TENT, Day was going over some intelligence. They planned on moving out from Talil and heading northwest to Nasiriyah, where there were supposed to be more of Saddam's forces. Day was speaking to a staff sergeant when the tent vent opened, interrupting him. Over his shoulder, he said, "Yes. What is it?"

"Sorry to interrupt, sir. It's just that Nima has some information for us."

"Nima?" He perked up like a rabbit. "Come right in."

Nima was the Iraqi interpreter's real name. He knew this country and these people better than anyone. Kurds from Northern Iraq, he and his family had lived under Saddam's reign of terror all of their lives. This job was Nima's chance to topple Saddam once and for all.

Despite the requirements of the job, he was a naturally quiet guy. That and the fact that his English was great, and he was willing to risk the lives of himself and his family, added to the prestige the mild-mannered twenty-year-old carried among the soldiers getting their first taste of war.

Private First Class Jonathan Rosenblatt had been the one to interrupt. The PFC went out of the tent for a second to grab Nima, and seconds later, Nima entered. Day smiled at the terp and, pointing to his mask, told him, "You can take that off in here, son. No one can see you."

Nima mumbled some words and apologetically began to take off his mask. He smiled and looked around, happy to give his face a chance to breathe. Without being asked, Day handed him a cold bottle of water. Nima drank nearly half the contents in two gulps.

Day stood by in silence, his way of telling Nima to proceed.

"Go on," said Rosenblatt. "Tell 'em what you told me."

With a quick nod to Rosenblatt, Nima turned to Lieutenant Day and said, "Mrs. Bousaid?"

"Yes, I'm aware of her. What about her?"

"Well, earlier today as I was on patrol, I saw that she was washing clothes with other women. We began to talk. After a few moments, she began to tell me that she sympathizes with us."

"How sure are you she's being truthful?"

"Not sure at all. Just relaying what she told me."

This brought a smile to Day's face. The Iraqi kid was smart. Taught himself a foreign language and everything. Before the war, he was one of the brightest in math in the entire country. And that was saying a lot—Iraq was filled with brilliant minds. For a moment, the lieutenant wondered if after the war, the kid would be interested in coming Stateside. *We could always use another bright mind.*

"She said that she does not want bloodshed," Nima continued. "That she knows Saddam's reign is over. And she wants to help us so things can get back to normal in the village. And she's ready to prove it."

"She's ready to prove it? How so?" he asked.

"All she said was that at the same time and place tomorrow, she will provide me with information."

This elicited a chin scratch from the lieutenant. "Hmmm. I don't like it. I want to like it, but I don't." Everyone stood in silence as Day thought for a moment. He could have asked what others in the room thought, but it seemed he wanted to handle this on his own. He took his time thinking. "Tell you what. Go ahead and meet with her tomorrow. We'll bring extra guys in case there's anything fishy."

"I don't want her husband and the others to

become aware that she is possibly helping us. Is there another way, without bringing so much suspicion?"

Day nodded. The kid was admirable, the lieutenant thought. But just because this Iraqi was willing to risk his life didn't mean Day was about to risk the lives of his men.

"Look, we'll have it so that two patrols just happen to show up at the same time. It'll look like nothing is out of the ordinary, and I'll feel better knowing you have more cover. Cool?"

"Yes! Cool!"

Before Nima left, he put his mask back on. It couldn't cover his smile, though. Funny, Day thought. This kid might have just set up his own death sentence and he couldn't be happier about it.

Maybe Day would figure this place out by the time the war was over. Maybe.

Chapter 3

JUAN BOCANEGRA WONDERED IF MORNING in the Iraqi desert felt anything like the Moon. Just a few years ago, in high school, Boca had learned that the Moon had no atmosphere to act as a buffer between the heat and the cold. That's how Iraq felt to him: freezing nights followed by blistering hot days.

Dawn and sunset were the best, temperature-wise. The little sweet spots as the temperature changed. A bit on the cool side, just as Boca liked it.

He wasn't sure how he was supposed to feel. This was war, yes, but times were different now. It wasn't like a few decades ago when some madman tried to conquer Europe; it wasn't like Operation Desert Storm, where another country was invaded. No, this was a preemptive war—a war to liberate a people from the shackles of their oppressor.

Part of Boca wanted to hate the people there. He for sure hated the place, but it was hard to hate old people, women, and children. Even the military-aged men got a small dose of pity from him. Those who fought did so because they had to. The rest were just trying to go about their lives and not bother anyone. Hating these people would make the job easier, but right now, today, he didn't.

He was still a little groggy. This was his first day trying to change from a night shift to a day shift, so he had barely gotten any sleep. Still, he felt good considering. The air was clean, his mind was in a good place, and the kids always lifted his spirits.

They were already out playing soccer. Since their little dirt field didn't have any night lights, these kids used up as much sunlight as possible. Boca enjoyed seeing this bit of normalcy in a tense situation, and having the kids around also meant that he and his men were safe for the time being.

One of the soldiers, Lance Corporal Lewis Parish, was playing some sort of mix of goalie and defender. The kids were running around him as he held his ground with one hand on his slinged M16. Parish was a bit goofy and somewhat quiet. The nice guy of the group. Everyone liked him, not so much because he was such an easygoing guy, but because he didn't tend to rub people the wrong way.

Just then, Boca felt as if someone was staring at him. He looked down to his left—he had company. The boy with the shirt dress from the previous night had snuck up on him and was standing there, staring.

"Hey, buddy."

The staff sergeant received no response. Boca returned the kid's stare. Shirt Dress stood there and played with his bottom lip.

Boca reached into one of his vest pockets and grabbed some candy. As he was bringing it up, Shirt Dress grabbed it from his hand and ran off a few feet.

"Little bastard," Boca murmured to himself with a smile. That was when it dawned on him. This kid probably really *was* a bastard. No father or mother ever came for him. The only one who looked after him seemed to be Zahida, and even she did so only in passing. Boca wasn't sure where Shirt Dress went at night. Maybe some other abandoned house the homeless kids lived in. A bit of guilt and sadness landed on his chest. It sure as heck stopped him from being mad at the kid for running off like a thief.

He was sitting down a mere five yards away now, eating his candy while looking up at Boca like a little squirrel.

The sergeant pulled out more candy. Shirt Dress continued to look. Boca half expected him to cock his head to the side like a puppy. But this kid was no animal, he reminded himself. Sure, Shirt Dress might not speak, but he was just as much a person as Boca was.

Shirt Dress got up off the ground, the prospect of more candy too enticing to pass up. His sticky hands were covered in dirt. He walked slowly back over to Bocanegra. Boca did everything he could to conceal how happy he was that his plan was working.

There they stood again, looking at each other. The kid went for the candy again, but Boca was ready this time. He pulled his hand away from the speedy would-be thief.

"Uh, uh, uh," Boca said, wagging one finger while the other hand wrapped around the candy. "You can take this, but slowly. Nice and easy, okay? Slow-ly." Boca gently put his arm back down, still gripping the candy. Then he opened his hand.

The kid was confused. He looked at the candy, then Boca, then the candy again. He made a quick grab but Boca closed his fist again. Shirt Dress wasn't liking this game. But it wasn't really a game; Boca wanted to show the kid some manners. He demonstrated with his other hand as he slowly went over and grabbed a piece of candy from his own hand. He then put the candy close to the kid's face.

Shirt Dress went fast again, and again Boca gestured to him to slow it down. Then the kid did just as Boca had wanted. He meticulously lifted his hand and placed into Boca's. He held the candy out for a second and then made eye contact. "See, that wasn't too hard. All you had to—"

The kid grabbed all the candy and ran off again. Boca chuckled. *He'll get it*, he thought. *Eventually.*

The radio on his shoulder came to life. He confirmed orders and looked over to Lance Corporal Parish.

"Yo, Parish. Let's get outta here. We gotta go by the well. Parish!"

Parish acted like he hadn't heard the first time, but the second call of his name meant he had no choice but to stop playing.

He came over to Bocanegra, smiling ear-to-ear. Boca wasn't sure who the biggest kid out there was, Shirt Dress or Parish.

IT TOOK them longer than usual to arrive at the waypoint. The road they had taken before was now filled with trash and furniture that had been dumped into the middle of the street. The villagers had begun to revolt. The gesture was small on the grand scale, but it was still poignant. It meant the troops were not welcome, and their stay wouldn't be easy.

Most of the mechanized infantry squad thought of it as a mere inconvenience—the town's way of shooting spit balls at the teacher. But it made Boca nervous. He knew the villagers were blocking their route in an attempt to lead them down another one. Perhaps they were trying to "smoke them out." Toward what, he didn't want to find out.

Boca might have had the best of intentions toward the villagers, but they likely did not share his feelings. Maybe he would get what he wanted after all and end up hating these people.

When they finally arrived at the well, it was bustling with activity. Women and children were all about, playing. A group of girls was sitting down, singing some sort of song that made them giggle at parts.

The unit assigned to the well consisted of two companies: Boca's Alpha and Grant's Bravo. Bravo company was already there—they'd arrived with Nima, the terp. They walked around and mingled with the kids. When Boca's company arrived, the two groups met up and started talking. Their paths were crossing casually, just as planned. They shared the usual boring pleasantries until Boca's radio ordered his Alpha company back to the square.

As he returned to his Humvee, one of the women came up to him and handed him a pillow. He looked at it, gave it a few squeezes, and handed it back to her, but she refused. It was hand-embroidered with some type of crochet. He turned around to the other squad lead, Staff Sergeant Micah Staniforth, who was also receiving a gift, this one a ceramic teakettle. They looked at each other, and then all around: all the women there were patiently waiting to see if they would take the gifts. From across the grounds, two NCOs looked at each other and nodded in agreement: they'd take the olive branches.

Staniforth walked over to Bocanegra and handed him the teapot.

"Take this back to camp for me, will ya?" Staniforth said.

"Oh, so I can be blown up by these booby traps?" Boca said.

Smiling, Staniforth said, "There's nothing in them."

Boca began to open the tea pot, but Staniforth shut it with his hands. He looked directly into Boca's eyes and said, slowly and deliberately, "There's nothing in them. Understand?"

He nodded even though he really didn't get it. Finally, Staniforth let go of the blue-and-white ceramic pot and left it in Boca's hands. He turned and walked away without saying another word.

"What the heck was that about?" Grant asked as he entered the vehicle.

Closing the Humvee's door and handing the items to Grant, Boca responded, "I don't know what that was." He took off his helmet to brush some sand out of his hair and then put it back on. He began to drive. "But I guess now we got some cool stuff to play tea party with." He turned, anticipating a laugh from his buddy that never came. Instead Grant was holding something new in his hand.

Still cradling the gifts, he had opened the pot and was holding up a yellow paper that had been inside of it.

Bocanegra briefly looked at him and the paper, then snatched it from his hand. He looked at it while trying to keep his eyes on the road. It was entirely in

Arabic and the paper was freshly folded. He stuffed it into his load-bearing vest and told Grant, "Looks like we were in the middle of an information drop op and we didn't even know it."

THE TENT FLAP opened and in came Nima. The Iraqi was quickly becoming Day's favorite soldier. He entered without saying a word and lifted the yellow piece of paper from the table. He read it silently, his head moving from right to left, while everyone waited.

Nima turned the paper over to see if there was anything else, but when he saw it was blank on the other side, he began to speak. "She says that most of the men that were here were foreigners. Most of them came through Iran, many Africans, and some Saudis. She even claimed there was an Italian among them."

"Foreign fighters," Day said, nodding in agreement. "We've heard Intel say that there are outside fighters coming into Iraq to perform their Jihad and die taking out as many Americans as possible." So far she was telling the truth, he thought.

"She also says that some men are going to attack the soldiers soon."

"When? Where?"

Looking at the paper again, the translator said, "She doesn't know when, but she says there are weapons stashed inside the house with yellow drapes."

"Bullshit," said a voice from the corner—Boca's. "We cleared this entire town. Every house has been searched from top to bottom and not a single weapon was found."

Holding up the paper as proof, Nima said, "That is not what she said."

Walking up to Nima, still not believing what he'd heard, Boca asked, "What house with yellow drapes?" There were several in town that he could remember.

Glancing at the paper, Nima said, "Next to the one with the garage door. No wait, the one *with* the garage door." Boca nodded. He knew the one. They had passed it today for the first time when their usual route was blocked. Interesting.

Turning to Bocanegra, Day said, "I need you to gather your men. Take an unmechanized squad. Go in and check this out. Not now—wait until nightfall."

"And if this is some elaborate trap?" Boca asked.

"Then it's an elaborate trap. I dunno. The fact that she knows about the foreign fighters makes me want to believe her."

"Yeah, but that news was leaking out already. Who's to say she's not just passing along old information as new to shiny up her resume?"

"You may be right. Only one way to find out, though."

Yeah, by me and my men kicking in doors and getting shot, Boca thought.

"If this doesn't pan out…" It took every ounce of patience not to burst out in anger. He calmly excused himself and walked out of the tent.

He was on the edge of something either very good or very bad. He wanted to believe that this woman was telling the truth; he wanted to believe that some of them were on their side. But another part of him—the majority of his being—felt otherwise. This had the makings of a massive ruse, and the players on this stage might not live to perform another show.

A LITTLE AFTER eleven o'clock Bocanegra and Staniforth began to prepare for the evening's raid. They'd strapped the armor extra tight and brought along a few more ammo drums. It would be full battle rattle for this one.

Aircrafts had been flying all week, so the noise of a reconnaissance helicopter would not surprise anyone. But just to be safe, the MH-6 Little Bird that was providing point hovered at a distance. To lessen the tail rotor noise as much as possible, it faced away from the town.

The MH-6, also known as the Killer Egg, could be both eyes and a weapon in combat. Tonight its role was for eyes only, but as in all combat situations, it was flexible.

Boca's Alpha team would breach the building while Staniforth's Bravo team covered the ground just outside. Earlier in the day, two Marines had taken cover in an abandoned building across from the target house, setting up a sniper's den. This was more for reconnaissance than anything; still, you could never have enough guns pointed at the bad guys.

The town was not all that old, but its design wasn't modern either. The passages between many buildings were only navigable by foot. The side of the house with the garage door was facing the street. The only other entrance was at back, a metallic door. The unit's objective, codenamed YELLOW, was somewhere between them.

It was a two-level building. The troops had cleared the house by entering the low windows in the rear, which had not been boarded up. On the top, all the windows were open, but they couldn't see inside because of the yellow curtains. So their only real option was to break the back windows and enter through there.

Staniforth's men waited across the street, looking at the front of the house. In case anyone ran down the main thoroughfare, they'd be there. Directly across from them were the snipers, playing eyes on YELLOW. And way up in the sky, staying in a stable hover, was the helo relaying the action back to Day.

At 2305 local, Alpha team began to make their way toward the target.

The first man there, Specialist Bryan Guinard, quietly placed a silhouette charge on the window frame. Lance Corporal Bret Bishop positioned himself next to the window and looked away. Guinard nodded to Boca, and Boca nodded back to indicate that the team was ready. The specialist clicked a switch and the explosives went off. It sounded like someone banging on a door, only louder. Glass fell and a dog barked in the distance. Not even the smoke was visible in the night. The bright flash was quick, and the soldiers had made sure to shield their eyes to preserve their night vision.

As soon as the glass broke, Guinard moved out of the way and Bishop hit the ground, getting on all fours right under the window. Alpha company began using him as a stepping stool to jump into the building. Inside, there were men lying down on mattresses.

"Hands up! Hands up!"

The Iraqis looked strange in the green tint of night vision. There were three of them on separate mattresses on the floor. Private First Class Joey Powis secured the men. Bishop and Grant climbed up the stairs with Bocanegra close behind.

As Grant turned up the stairs, he saw the door to the second floor room close abruptly. Like an enraged bull, Grant bolted up those stairs, ready to kick the door in. As soon as he reached it, he was so full of adrenaline and anger that he decided to use his shoulder to breach the entryway. His decision was the right one: the door boomed off and flew into the room.

"Hands up! Hands up!"

The men inside the room didn't have time to reach for their weapons.

Across the room, lined up against the wall, were five AK-47s.

"SO WHAT DO YA THINK?" Boca asked.

"What do I think?" Day sounded incredulous, "I think the op was a success and that she's telling the truth."

"This might just be a clever way to get us to trust her," Boca insisted, knowing it was unlikely but still feeling like he had to bring it up. All possibilities had to be put on the table, no matter how small or ridiculous they might seem.

"Yeah, there are a million different possibilities, but not acting on any of them isn't a choice I'm about to make. Plus"—he opened the tent's flap to show what was happening outside—"if she, or anyone else, does double cross us, they'll have that to deal with."

Outside the makeshift headquarters, an M113 Armored Personal Carrier had finally arrived. This time, instead of bringing troops into the village, it was empty, ready to be filled with human cargo. There were five men in total, all hooded, with Flexi-Cuffs around their wrists. They were being sent to an undisclosed prison. The entire village watched as they were loaded onto the vehicle. If this wasn't a deterrent, Boca wasn't sure what was.

Everything had changed, yet at the same time nothing was different. Boca wasn't sure what this meant in the greater scheme of things. All he knew for sure was that he was ready to see this whole thing through, no matter where it led him.

DAY MET with the sheik inside his house. "Thank you for having us," he said, and Nima translated.

"I had no choice."

"That is correct," said the American lieutenant, "But still, thank you for having us. Makes everything easier when people cooperate, don't you think?"

Bousaid's house was nothing to write home about. He might have been the town sheik, but his house was no better or worse than anyone else's. It was more a collection of rooms with dirt floors than anything. Day wasn't sure what the walls were made of—stucco probably—but it was cool inside even if there wasn't any air conditioning. The walls were painted Smurf blue in a sorry attempt to liven up the space. It made the place all the more odd. There were no chairs in the room, so they all sat on the ground. There was a TV in one corner, and a black-and-white photo of some old man on the wall. Besides that, nothing.

Day continued, "Why didn't you tell us about the weapons stash?" He stared at Bousaid with a smile as he waited for the translation.

With that ever-annoyed expression, Bousaid said, "Of course I didn't know. How am I supposed to know what everyone inside this village does? I'm only one man."

"Oh, cut the crap, Mufaddal," Day said. "No one in this town can so much as fart without your permission, and you're gonna tell me you had no idea that your people were hiding weapons? Come on now. Where are the other weapons?"

"I don't know."

"Well, you wanna know what *I* know? Those five bad guys we got going to who-knows-where are gonna be talking soon. And unless you want to join them, I suggest you start being more cooperative. For our sake and yours."

"They won't say anything," Bousaid said defiantly.

"They won't say anything because they know something?"

"I've told you. I knew nothing and I know nothing. Stop wasting our time."

Just then, Zahida came in with tea. Sheik Bousaid seemed surprised at this development. He started scolding her and brushing her off. Day didn't think it was possible, but he seemed to hate this man more every minute.

As the wife left, Day realized the only people in the room were male. The daughters were in the other room, looking in. The sheik had his young son, Salih, next to him. He must have been all of nine years old.

As Day stood, so did everyone else in the room. "Have it your way," he said. "*When* these guys start talking, if they say you had even the smallest bit of knowledge of what they were up to, I'll make sure you're on the first transport out to join them."

Bousaid was not so cocky now. He nodded quickly in agreement.

Day and his men walked out. As they headed to the Humvee, Staniforth asked, "D'ya think they're planning anything else?"

"I'm sure they are." He stopped and looked around. All Day saw was a wasted town. This good-for-nothing dirt trap was probably where he would die. There was no comfort in that.

LATER THAT DAY, Bravo company saw one of Bousaid's daughters come out and feed some of the children. There was no sign of Zahida.

As the little girl finished and reentered her house, Lance Corporal Lewis Parish briefly caught a glimpse of the sheik's wife in the doorway. She covered her face well, but not well enough to cover the bruising over her right eye. How bad the rest of her face had been beaten was anyone's guess.

AFTER THE DUAL spectacles of the men being sent off to jail and the meeting with the sheik, things slowly returned to normal.

Word was that they were to move out soon. Good, Bocanegra thought. A good old-fashioned fight would be better than standing around that ghost town waiting to get shot. There was an eerie calm as everyone returned to business as usual. As always, Shirt Dress hovered around. Knowing he wouldn't get a response, Boca asked the kid, "What's your name?"

"His name is Alli," a voice said from behind him.

Boca quickly turned around. He kept his weapon down, because the voice was a child's. He realized it was Bousaid's son, Salih.

"Well, why doesn't he talk? Doesn't he like Americans?"

"He no talk to no one. And he also hate America. We all hate America."

Boca nodded his head. "So what's your story, little man?"

"What is my what?"

The kid's English went only so far. Boca decided to communicate the best way he knew how: he grabbed some candy.

Alli—Shirt Dress—was of course the first one to take some candy. Boca gave him about half and Salih the rest. Then he looked at both kids and placed two fingers to his eyes, motioning for the kids to watch. He pointed at Sergeant Grant, who was watching the other kids playing soccer.

He slowly crept up to Grant, exaggerating his walk. Knowing that he was up to something, the two boys covered their mouths, trying not to laugh. Boca kicked the back of Grant's left knee, making his leg buckle, and pulled on his belt at the same time. Grant came flying down and landed on his back in the sand, eliciting a cloud of dirt and a burst of laughter from the children. He jumped up and got right in Boca's face. "What gives, man!"

Guinard quickly came over and broke them up. Grant walked away, turning to give Boca one final scowl.

Boca returned to the Iraqi kids, who were giving him the thumbs-up. Just then Alli pointed in shock, as if something was happening right behind Boca. Boca turned, half expecting to find Grant having a second go at him, but was instead treated to a kick on the back of his knee.

"Oh, you little bastards!" he shouted, though the kick wasn't enough to knock him over. He gave chase to the laughing, fleeing children. He caught up to Salih and kicked his feet out from under him. The kid came crashing down to the ground, face down.

What have I done? Boca thought. In a moment of youthful exuberance, he had just kicked a kid to the ground. And not just any kid, but the damn sheik's son. Just when he was thinking about the dishonorable discharge he was going to get for knocking down a minor, Salih turned and got up, laughing. The kid didn't seem to care. In fact, he seemed to enjoy it.

Back in America, Boca might've been arrested and sued. Here, it seemed, the kids didn't mind a little roughhousing.

Boca wasn't going to risk getting overly physical again, however, so he quickly went over to a flattened soccer ball and kicked it to the kids. They spent the next hour running around kicking a flat ball at each other.

Boca couldn't remember the last time he'd had so much fun. Maybe it was so fun because it helped him forget where he was.

THAT EVENING, things grew even more quiet around town. The stars were out, but the moon was hidden. It was about time for bed, but Bravo's Parish had found some smokes and was sharing them with Boca. In the dead of night, with no sound at all, it was easy to feel as if they were all alone in the middle of nowhere. But they weren't.

"So, did ya hear?" Parish asked.

"Hear what?" Boca said.

"That we're leaving here soon, moving on up to Nasiriyah."

"Yeah, I heard that," Boca said as he stubbed out his cigarette. He rarely had one, but sometimes he needed something to break up the monotony of the day. "I've heard lots of things. I've heard Saddam's been caught too."

They both laughed. It was weeks into the invasion, and the ace of spades had yet to be captured.

"Well, I'm for sure leaving."

"Oh yeah?" This brought a slight smile to Boca's face. "And tell me just how it is you're gonna do that?"

"All right. I'm not *leaving* leaving. Just leaving."

"What the hell are you talking about?" The first things to pop into Boca's mind were Parish going AWOL or committing suicide, but neither of those fit the guy's character.

"I'm going out on an escort run."

Boca nodded. He understood now. Parish explained he was going out to accompany a convoy from Talil Air Base back to the town.

"What's coming in?"

"Same ol' same: a water tanker, supplies, fuel. The norm."

But no troops, thought Boca. If there were troops

coming along, there would be no need for Parish to help provide transport security. He felt he had to ask anyway.

"Aren't they bringing in any more Marines? We could use some relief."

"Naw, if they were bringing in more guys you'd think they'd be having us go out there? Plus, it's not like we'll be going out alone."

"What do ya mean?"

"We're not going all the way out to the airport. We're meeting them a few clicks out from there. They'll transfer security over to us at that point," Parish said.

"Kind of like passing the baton, huh?"

Parish laughed. "Yeah, I guess you could say that."

"When do you guys leave?"

"Tomorrow night."

"Tomorrow night?"

"Yes, sir. We leave here around 2300. Hoping to meet the convoy around midnight and be back by 0100. My first command." Parish beamed when he said it. "Taking Bravo company out while Staniforth sleeps and sucks his thumb."

As they shared a silent laugh, they heard something on the other side of the Humvee. After giving each other a quizzical look, they went around to the other side of the vehicle. There he was: the kid, Shirt Dress Alli. As soon as he saw the pair, he got up and ran.

"Shit!" Parish said. "Where'd that little bastard go?"

"Relax." Boca put his hand on Parish's shoulder, knowing what he was thinking. "He doesn't speak or understand a word of English."

"Ya sure?"

"Yeah, I'm sure." But as soon as Boca had said it, he realized he wasn't sure at all.

Chapter 4

THE DRIVER WAS STILL FRIGHTENED. An hour ago, he was driving another vehicle—albeit a different one—yet he had been scared out of his mind then, too.

Then, as now, the driver white-knuckled the steering wheel. He wasn't sure if he should go forward with what he had agreed to. But he'd made it through then, and he was here now.

While driving earlier that evening, he was amazed that he had made it out of his house. He didn't hide his nervousness well from his family. He felt a bit guilty that his wife's last memory of him would be a brief argument. But it was for her own good. All of this was for his family's good, he kept telling himself. He prayed that one day they would understand, hopefully sooner than later.

He had lain in bed, sweating through the sheets, staring at the clock on the wall. It was one of those unlit analog clocks, but his eyes were so adapted to the dark from not sleeping that he was able to see it clearly. He was supposed to wake up at ten and meet at the designated location by ten-thirty. But he knew he wouldn't need to set an alarm. He wouldn't be getting a wink of sleep on his last night alive.

A little after nine, the driver couldn't take the waiting anymore. He got up and left the room. As he cracked his bedroom door open one last time, a rectangular block of light illuminated his wife's back. She was sound asleep. He thought about how much he loved her, and quietly closed the door behind him.

He entered his children's room. All four were asleep. One bunk bed and two mattresses on the floor. He kissed the forehead of the nearest child, his oldest, a girl.

And then he was off in his car. He had felt like he wasn't even breathing. He was nervous and second-guessing his agreement to go on the mission. He wanted to do it, but there were different parts of his own mind that fought each other—the old fight-or-flight trick. He did everything in his power not to run, even though every cell in his being screamed at him to turn back. He was thirsty. The directions they gave him were confusing. He was a ball of nerves. Most people wish for a quiet, happy death; his would be anything but.

Then a bright light brought him back to reality, back to the here and now. Someone had illuminated him and the truck by turning on an unseen vehicle's headlights. One of the men opened the door to the truck. The man had the same beard and AK-47 as always, but this time, he carried something he had never displayed before: a smile.

"Today is a glorious day, brother," the bearded man said. The terrified driver in the truck nodded quickly. It was hard to see the bearded man, since he was silhouetted by the parked car's blinding headlights.

A second man came and handed the beard a plastic water bottle. He briefly looked at the driver. The beard handed the bottle to the driver, who drank it all almost instantly.

The beard breathed a laugh through his nose. Handing the empty water bottle back, the driver retuned a forced smile from the truck's cabin.

He was no longer in his car, of course. He was

inside a small, blue Toyota truck. He had never seen it before. Today, he would die in it.

Past the beard, he watched the assistant come back again. This time he was holding a camcorder. Someone inside the car turned off the headlights. The sudden change to darkness was oddly disorienting. As the driver got his bearings back, he noticed that the only light source was coming from the top of the video camera. The beard slammed the old truck's door shut.

As the beard walked back, he started to speak aloud. It was mainly for the camera. "Here you see a man of courage and bravery! A man who will not bow to the oppressive invaders!"

The cameraman then came right up to the truck's window. As if on cue, the driver said, "To my wife and children, I hope you understand what I am doing. It is good and just. I do this out of love for you."

LATER, a video showing a mustached man behind the wheel of a Toyota truck would appear on the Internet.

He appeared to be covered in sweat as he asked

for his family's understanding. The camera stayed on him as he turned his head to look forward. After a while, the camera faced the ground and the screen went blank. Just as quickly, the screen came back on. It wasn't clear exactly how much time had passed, but the brake lights of the truck were fading off against the dark horizon. To the right, in the distance, more headlights came on screen.

Everything became quiet. The headlights were still entering the frame to the right. At some point, the convoy must have noticed the truck coming at them, even though it had its headlights off. What happened next happened very quickly. Some type of machine gun fire came from the top of a vehicle with headlights. Nervous chatter came from those filming. Suddenly the night was illuminated: white light, then yellow, then finally an orange light that ballooned into the air, pierced by the thunder of the explosion. Off-camera, men could be heard cheering.

"LET'S GO! LET'S GO!" Specialist Bryan Guinard entered the makeshift barracks inside one of the abandoned houses, clapping his hands. He was the night watchman.

"What's going on?" Boca asked no one in particular. Of course, his first decent night's rest would be the one interrupted. When the watchman saw that most of the men were up, he answered the question on all their minds.

"Convoy Bravo has been hit. We've been asked to assess and assist in the situation."

Shit, Boca thought. *They attacked Parish*. Had the kid overheard them? It wasn't important right now. He needed to suit up and help one of his brothers. He'd deal with that shirt dress-wearing bastard when he got back.

IN THE DISTANCE, Boca could see the glow. Whatever they'd used, it had packed quite a wallop. The entire scene was lit up by the flames. As suspected, the fuel tanker had been breached and it was lighting up the sky like a bonfire.

In any normal convoy, there would be a Humvee at the front. But it wasn't there. They found only a crater followed by the mangled fuel tanker.

Then, in the distance, they found the Humvee. It

was about twenty yards away, shrouded in darkness. There were men already there guarding it. It was strange for it to be so far away from the convoy, but maybe it had tried to flee or move around to a better attack position.

Boca was stopped by another Marine on guard. "Sorry, sir. We're trying to keep this area free for the investigators."

"Investigators? Why? What's wrong?"

As he awaited the Marine's response, he saw that the Humvee he had thought was intact was actually heavily damaged.

"Vehicle one was blown and rolled several times, and landed over here. The bomber had his vehicle filled with shrapnel. Everyone inside was KIA." Killed in action. When Boca heard that, he knew they were no longer a fighting force as much as they were on a recovery mission—a mission to recover the bodies of his friends.

The left side had buckled. The Humvee was riddled with not so much holes, but slashes. Like a knife had sliced through the metal.

Boca wasn't about to argue with the Marine. He was happy for a reason not to go over there. He didn't have any desire to see his friends mauled up.

He'd remember them as they were, not as they'd been ended. He would mourn later.

After he walked back to patrol, Guinard informed him of what happened.

"At about 0030, the convoy was hit by a suicide bomber. Bravo team was able to shoot the oncoming vehicle; however, it continued to roll with the dead man behind the wheel. It must have been a timed fuse because it continued to roll toward the convoy, exploding near the front. Parish's team and the fuel tank driver were instantly killed. The other men hunkered down and protected the convoy from any further attack. Thank goodness it never came."

Stopping and protecting the convoy had been the correct call this time around. Usually, the order would have been to keep moving, but since the road was taken out and they were surrounded by darkness, holding their ground and waiting for friendlies was a better option than running blind.

As Boca helped to secure the perimeter, he felt something he never thought he'd feel: betrayed. He had been a fool to think his enemies were his friends. He wasn't lulled into this false sense of comfort by any outside force, but by his own wishful thinking. He felt betrayed by the village, but more so, he felt as if he'd deceived himself for being so trusting.

All he could see in front of him was darkness. Somewhere out there, though, were the men responsible for this. They were watching him, and without a doubt, enjoying what they saw.

THE SKY WAS TURNING SLIGHTLY purple as Boca got back into town.

He felt as if he hadn't blinked in hours. His head was throbbing with anger. He tasted blood from having his teeth clenched so hard. When others tried to make small talk on the ride back, he didn't say a word. He was full-on pissed, but he had to bottle up his wrath.

He wasn't sure who he was going to let loose on first— Bousaid or the kid. One thing was for sure: he was going to let one or both of them have it.

As soon as they stopped, he jumped out of the transport and walked over to the nearest soldier, Rosenblatt. "Where is he?"

"Who?" Rosenblatt asked.

"Bousaid." It was the first name that came to his lips. It made sense. Even though he was sure the kid brought the intel for the attack, it was the sheik who put that night's tragic events into motion.

"They got him near HQ. Don't you worry, my man; he's being questioned and dealt with thoroughly."

Boca nodded. Knowing someone was chewing out the sheik made him feel better, even if he wasn't the one doing it.

"They're also questioning him about the in-town casualty."

"Casualty?"

Rosenblatt had brought it up to see if Boca had heard. He obviously hadn't. "They found a civilian casualty in one of the alleyways."

"Where?"

Rosenblatt told him.

Without another word, Boca started walking.

A two-man team was there, keeping watch. They were laughing about something.

"What's shakin', my man?" one of the men asked as Boca approached.

Boca felt these guys were a little too jovial for having just lost some of their friends, but then he had to remind himself that people dealt with things differently. Boca responded with, "What do we got?"

"One of the little Hajis. Someone stuck him in

the neck. Bled out like the pig he was." This got a laugh from the other Marines. They were dealing with the news of their dead comrades like soldiers had done for hundreds of years: by celebrating the death of an enemy.

As Bocanegra moved past the soldiers, he saw the dead body. It was Alli. His eyes were wide open, and his shirt dress was covered in blood.

Chapter 5

THEY BOTH JUST SAT THERE, puffing on their cigarettes, letting the room fill with smoke. They were sitting on the floor, both looking into nothingness.

"Ain't right," Grant said, slowly shaking his head. "Ain't right at all."

Boca nodded. Several lives had been lost, all of them good men. Even the Iraqi fuel tank driver inside the convoy. Word got around that the fuel tank driver had lied to his wife and told her he was visiting his sick mother. He actually went to do one last convoy run for the Americans for a little extra cash. Instead, he was dead. They all were.

Boca silently brooded about Alli. He didn't have to die. Boca had never heard a word from the kid, yet he still liked him. He gave up the information on the Americans, and how'd they thank him? By putting a pipe in his neck so he wouldn't talk. This place was disgusting. Horrible. The sense of what was right and wrong wasn't as clear here as it was back home. He hated this country. He hated that his friends were dead. He hated that Shirt Dress Alli was dead. He even hated that he hated that Alli was dead.

"We gotta do something," Grant said.

"Do what?"

"I dunno…" He paused for a second and nodded. "Just something."

Lieutenant Day came in. He could sense the dread through the cigarette smoke.

"Look, guys, I'm not gonna try to sugarcoat this shit. We all lost a friend out there today. We're all a little frazzled." He waited for a response. There was none. He continued, "I do have some good news on this clusterfuck of a day, however." This got both men's attention from the ground up to Day's eyes. "We're outta here. We're leaving."

"When?" No one was more surprised to hear Boca's voice than Boca.

"Day after tomorrow. Saturday."

Everyone shared a glance. Since Boca was

suddenly in a chatty mood, he continued, "And what about the sheik?"

"What about him? We already let him go."

Grant leapt off the ground. "Bullshit! What the fuck are you talking about? He's the reason our men are dead!" Realizing he might have gone too far, Grant stepped back and took a breath.

The lieutenant put his hands up in a request for calm. "Marine, no one is happy about this. But no one's talking. What else could we do?" Now it was his turn to stare at the ground. After a moment, he lifted his head and made eye contact with Grant again. "No one is gonna pick these guys up as POWs right now. All our forces are moving out, and that includes us. When the war dies down and the dust starts to settle, this guy will get his day. But today is not that day."

Grant sulked. He couldn't believe what he was hearing. This was some type of PC crap, he was sure of it. He stood there, wide-eyed, with both hands on his hips. He sucked in his cheeks and sat back down on the ground. With his legs crossed at the ankles and his elbows on his knees, he looked like a child whose bike had just been stolen.

"Look, guys, we're getting outta here. That's the good news. Don't forget that. One step closer to

Baghdad is one step closer to home, okay?" He took the silence as an affirmative. As Day walked out, he said without looking at them, "Start packing up and get ready to head out. I, for one, can't wait to get into a decent battle and away from this fuckin' town."

The tent vent closed.

Chapter 6

"SO WHAT ARE YOU PLANNING on doing?" Boca asked Grant.

"You really wanna know?"

Boca shook his head no. He didn't have the courage to look into Grant's eyes. Boca was torn—he didn't necessarily want to kill the sheik. Okay, that was a lie. He did want to kill the man. It was what the sheik deserved. Boca just didn't want to risk his life or wind up in a military prison. It wasn't worth the risk.

Then he thought of Alli, and Parish, and he knew he had to help Grant with the mission.

Grant's mind was already made up. He was going to kill Bousaid and there was nothing anyone, let alone Bocanegra, could do to stop him. Grant could go it alone, but it would work better if he had an extra pair of eyes.

Boca reasoned that if Grant was going to do it anyway, he might as well make sure he did it right and as safely as possible.

As quiet as possible, they got their equipment together next to Grant's Bradley tank. Grant whispered to Boca with a slight grin, "I'll be right back." Then he returned from the inside of the Brad holding something white and wearing a smile.

"I've had this since we first got boots on ground," he held it up to Boca to see. "I found it in a garage and took it. Never knew when or if I'd ever need it. Perfect for tonight, though."

It was a white fuel filter. Designed for a car, this little automotive part also had an unintended use: It had the exact same grove markings to fit a standard issue Beretta. It was a near perfect silencer. The first shot would be a whisper, but after that, the can would be breached and the following gunshots would become increasingly louder, though they would still be muffled.

During battle, sound suppression was a bad idea.

For one, it slowed down the round and made it more inaccurate. In nearly all close-range contact, it didn't really make a difference, since the bullet was still flying at a lethal speed. But in battle, distance mattered.

Plus, the noise of battle was a good thing. Giving away your position was encouraged, because it helped define the battle line—who was a friendly and who was an enemy. During the World Wars, fighter planes and tanks had insignias for that very purpose. Today, the repeating bangs of either an M16 or AK47 marked the belligerents.

But tonight, none of that mattered. This was not a battle between two enemy countries. This was an assassination.

THEY HAD MADE it about a block away from the sheik's house undetected. They stopped and gathered themselves for one last moment.

Even though they were running on training, this felt different. It was different. Under international law, they were about to commit a war crime. They both knew it, but their consciousness wouldn't allow it to surface. They were both breathing heavy.

"You got me?"

Boca acknowledged Grant's smile with his own. "I got you."

Grant screwed the air filter onto the end of his firearm. Against the dark of night, the white can stood out like a sore thumb. Boca thought they probably should've covered it in electrical tape, or at least painted it with a marker or something, but it was too late for any of that.

After placing the makeshift silencer on his gun, Grant made sure a small burlap bag was placed securely around the gun. For obvious reasons, the Marines didn't issue brass catchers. But tonight, they weren't acting on the Marines' orders. They were acting on their own. The bag had been found inside one of the abandoned houses. It was the kind of thing the Iraqis might use as a purse, or a hippie back home would shop with. Tonight, it had the job of catching hot brass that had once been filled with gunpowder and tipped with lead. There would be no trace of their visit.

Boca handed Grant a makeshift mask. He looked at it for a moment, then handed it back to Boca.

"You're not gonna put it on?"

"No. It's pretty obvious an American is going in there," he said, gesturing to his body.

"But—"

"Dude, don't worry," Grant assured him, "Plus, the only person who's gonna see me isn't gonna be able to share what I did to him."

They exchanged a grin.

Grant closed his eyes and took a deep breath in. He slowly exhaled and opened his eyes. He nodded to Boca. Boca nodded back. And with that, Grant was off.

IT WAS STRANGE, Boca thought. Here he was, keeping watch, like he had done plenty of times. Only this time, he was keeping an eye out for everyone—both bad guys and good guys. If anyone got wind of what they were attempting, they'd be in a world of trouble. It was the first and probably only time in his life he'd rather run into a bad guy than one of his own men.

As always in battle, Boca's every sense was heightened. The smallest noise sounded like a thunderclap. He felt as if the whole world could hear the sound of his gear brushing against him.

Then he heard something else, like a snapping. Then he heard it again. And again. A few more times, increasingly louder. Then silence. Out of the corner came Grant, running. Half surprised, Boca ran up and joined him.

"Did ya get 'im?"

Stopping to toss the canister atop a house, Grant looked at Boca. "Yeah, we got 'em."

Chapter 7

I T WAS A DUSTY MORNING. The winds were kicking up, and with all the equipment moving, the town was filled with a dirty brown fog.

All Boca knew was that he wanted out. Grant had killed the bastard in cold blood last night, and Boca hadn't slept a wink. Grant, on the other hand, seemed well-rested and had an extra hop in his step.

Strange, Boca thought. It should've been the other way around. Grant was the one who killed the guy. So why was it eating him up so much? They were built differently; that was why. Boca had a conscience. He hated that about himself. It did him no good out in this forsaken desert. But you could never cover up who you really were, no matter how much you tried to tell yourself otherwise.

"We found 'em," Day said, interrupting his thoughts.

"Found who, sir?" Boca had to yell over the noise of the vehicles and wind.

The lieutenant responded, "The family. Bousaid and his family."

"What about his family?" Boca was afraid of the answer.

"Him, his wife, both daughters. All shot to death."

Boca felt his mouth start to dry up. The news had made his jaw drop and he was standing there, staring.

It was hard for Day to gauge Boca's reaction, because the dirt-covered goggles obscured his eyes.

"Just get your men and get outta here," Day commanded.

"Right."

"We'll deal with this some other time," the LT said to no one in particular.

As Boca put the final items into the Brad, he looked out at the town square. Everyone was there. It was a strange sendoff, much like their welcoming. Not an angry one or a happy one, but one of indifference. It was like the townspeople were watching a train pass by. There was nothing they could do but wait it out.

Behind the cloud of dust, Boca saw Salih, the sheik's son. This gave him a slight sense of relief. At least someone had survived Grant's massacre. Salih was being held by a man, probably an uncle. They both looked right at him Boca.

Boca's happiness shifted to uneasiness. That kid would one day grow up and seek revenge. One day, that kid would be a man, a man whose mother, father, and sisters had been taken from him. Who knew? He was more than likely the one who discovered their dead bodies. Boca felt an immense regret and the need to leave overwhelmed him.

"Let's move out!"

Boca put himself into the Humvee. The other men entered. The driver, PFC Joey Powis, had a smile on his face. He looked over at Boca and his demeanor quickly changed. "You okay, sir?"

"Yeah, I'm fine. Let's just get the hell outta here."

"Yessir."

As the convoy left, another witness looked on. This inanimate object, unable to speak in words, lay upon the rooftop. It was a white canister with gaping bullet holes. It slowly rocked back and forth as the wind blew across the roof. It had a story to tell, and one day, it would have the opportunity.

CONDITION OF ANONYMITY

Chapter 1

"SO HOW DID YOU FIND ME?"

That earned a silent chuckle from Stewart Chinnery. "How didn't I find you?"

They exchanged a small grin. Stewart worked for the NSA—the National Security Agency. They were inside the home of Stewart's mother. It had all the trappings of an older women's home: Porcelain figurines dotted the walls, frozen in time. Doilies covered every table like white spider webs.

Stewart sat on an old chair with claw feet. The seat was upholstered in a floral print. With Stewart's youthful appearance, he might have been mistaken for a child visiting his grandmother's house, not his mother's.

A young man in his midtwenties, Stewart was

lanky and awkward. His face shared those attributes: his skull seemed stretched, making his face more egg-shaped than round. His disheveled hair exaggerated his features.

Stewart's thick glasses and bad skin added to his nerdy look. Either his tucked-in polo shirt was an embracement of this, or just another piece of evidence revealing how truly unconcerned he was about his appearance.

Across from him was the man who'd asked the question, Martin Sherratt. Martin had begun to judge Stewart's appearance before realizing he wasn't so different.

Martin had on tan pants and a light blue long-sleeved shirt. Underneath he wore a white t-shirt that hugged his neck like a priest's collar. He wore slip-on brown shoes, which were the extent of his attempt at fashion.

Stewart's hair was fair, while Martin's was dark. They shared pale complexions, however, and both probably could have used advice on their choice of glasses. Neither of them did much heavy lifting beyond moving computers around.

What had brought these two men together now, in this home that seemed frozen in time, was Stewart's job.

Ever since the Edward Snowden affair that gripped America and the world in 2013, the NSA had gone from a little-known organization to being front-page news. In response, the American government had cracked down on all possible whistleblowers with fines and penalties. Any leak that was deemed a risk to American security—and the new language was vague enough to cast a wide net—would be met with severe consequences. Now the world knew that the NSA knew everything about everyone. How and what, exactly, was still a mystery to many. Martin was hoping Stewart might be able to shine some light on that.

"I had to approach you the way I did. There was no other way," Stewart said, vaguely making eye contact.

"Yeah, no, I get that. But how'd you do it exactly?" Martin asked.

Martin was a reporter for the *New York Tribune*. He handled politics from the nation's capital. He had his reservations about being here; it wasn't unlike these Washington intelligence types to put the media on a false lead, and Martin was skeptical about today's meeting. He might be on one of those wild goose chases at this very moment.

Still, Martin held out some hope that there

might be something for him here. Even with the advent of the Department of Homeland Security, through which all major government agencies now shared information instead of keeping it from one another, there remained some barriers between groups. These self-created walls were ones no politician could ever really break down.

And where there were borders, imaginary or not, there was conflict. And every so often these groups liked to pit themselves against each other.

Better yet, maybe Stewart had something to give up about his own people, the NSA. That, Martin thought, would be a dream come true. A man could dream, couldn't he?

"Don't worry about that," Stewart said with a toss of his wrist and a soundless giggle. "That's small potatoes compared to what I'm going to give you."

"If it's small potatoes, why don't you just tell me what it is?"

This garnered an annoyed smile. "Do you want to hear me out or not?"

"Yeah, of course," Martin said. He might have been playing it too aggressive. "Although I'm not even sure what we're going to talk about."

"If you knew already, we wouldn't be here."

Martin didn't know exactly how to take that. He

didn't know how to take any of it. The initial exchange was pleasant enough. For the possible enormity that lay ahead, they were both surprisingly relaxed and happy.

"It's about a program we have. We call it CANDLESTICK," Stewart said.

We meant the NSA. Maybe dreams did come true. "What's CANDLESTICK?" Martin asked.

"CANDLESTICK isn't a thing or a single program in the usual sense. It's more of a group of programs that focuses on one mission."

"And that mission is?"

"Gathering personal information from Americans to possibly use against them in the future. To blackmail them."

Martin nodded. He wasn't sure if his dream had come true or if a nightmare was just about to begin.

THAT EVENING, over a few beers and a microwaved pizza, Stewart covered everything he knew about CANDLESTICK.

CANDLESTICK was the unofficial name the guys in the NSA had given the program. In reality, these different programs had different names that changed all the time. At least every one to three times a month, the names would be revised. As of that moment, the main components were called A85 and C105GG.

A85 was a system that used backdoor computer software algorithms. This system had the ability to track information about people from their computers or smartphones.

Besides the obvious things, like geolocation and web browser history, A85 was able to extract a wide range of information from any computer system. Its main purpose was to capture images and videos from these devices' cameras, unbeknownst to the participant.

It was a simple algorithm: First, a pattern for the target individual was determined. Everyone keeps a schedule, especially when doing things they might not want others to know about.

Most of these activities were sexual in nature; everything from looking at lurid websites to engaging in lurid acts via the Internet connection. All of it was documented and collected by A85.

C105GG was where this information was put into use. It was outside of Stewart's expertise, but he knew quite a bit about it since his program, A85, was dependent on it. C105GG was basically a blueprint of how to best use the information gained from A85, if it was ever deemed necessary. C105GG was once implemented when a certain congressman claimed he had sent someone a private photo over a social media platform. The media had caught wind of the indiscretion even though the then-congressman erased the message. He resigned in disgrace.

"But what you're saying is, he actually *did* send the message in private?" Martin asked, stunned by what he was hearing.

"Yes."

"But you then made it look like he posted it publicly?"

"Yes."

Martin knew he should have had another question. He had dozens, really. But he was in such shock that something like this could even happen that all he could do for a few moments was sit there agape.

"Is this even legal?" he finally managed.

"Please, Martin." Stewart rolled his eyes. "Whether what we do is legal or not is not our concern. We are given a job and then we do it. That's it."

Martin nodded and was about to say something when Stewart continued, "But yeah, off the record, this shit has to be a hundred percent illegal."

Again Martin was at a loss for words. Without even thinking, he asked, "So why are you telling me this? Why now?"

"Yeah, I knew that would be the big question. Well, the real big question should be why we have a multimillion-dollar system set up to spy on our citizens with the sole purpose of possibly blackmailing them.

"But that's not the only reason I want this brought to light. There are several, really. I hate my job and the people I work with. CANDLESTICK is a terrible program that should be shut down, yes, but I could also use the money. I'm thinking I write a book and retire in Russia or Cuba. Atone for my sins."

"Yeah, a Cuban wife and millions in your pocket. That's really a way to make good on your wrongs."

"You know what I mean."

"Yeah, I know. I know." Martin let out a short, nervous laugh. "So what do you need from me?"

"To be a reporter, of course. Spread the news. That kind of thing."

"Yeah. That kind of thing."

They chatted a few more minutes about the logistics. Martin was afraid Stewart was going to need some type of help getting out of the country or making contacts, but it turned out he had all of that already. All that was left to be done was getting the story out.

"I also need something from you," Martin said.

"Oh?"

It wasn't Martin's place to be too pushy, since Stewart held all the cards, but he couldn't let Stewart think he was going to be the only one calling the shots. "I can't just go off your word and your word alone. I'll need documents. Proof."

"I thought you might ask that. Wanted to make sure we were a good match before I handed anything over. That, and I needed to see if you were an NSA plant."

"An NSA plant? How could I know what you were going to tell me? You contacted *me*. Not the other way around. How could I possibly be a plant?"

"In my line of work, everyone knows what everyone else is doing all the time. Kind of refreshing to be with someone who doesn't know what's happening.

"Like a news reporter."

Chapter 2

MARTIN SHERRATT HAD BEEN WAITING to hear back from Stewart Chinnery after their initial meeting. They had agreed to meet two days later in a predetermined area: a supermarket parking lot. But Stewart never came. Although Martin had never called or emailed him, they had exchanged numbers and contact information in case of an emergency. Martin felt this qualified as one, and called and texted Stewart several times. All came back unanswered.

Finding him wouldn't be that hard. Martin knew his name and his place of work, obviously. Martin wasn't about to go to the NSA for obvious reasons, but he looked Stewart up the way most reporters did: by calling local hospitals and the county morgue. He found Stewart at the latter.

Oddly enough, the only address they had listed for Stewart was the one Martin had already been to —Stewart's mother's house.

When Martin returned to Stewart's mother's home, it was no longer empty of people. Mourners had gathered; mostly older folks, more likely there to comfort the grieving mother than to mourn a deceased friend.

In the face of death, people become more trusting, even as common sense says it should be the other way around. It seemed to Martin that maybe there was some force out there that already had everything written—that there were some rules in this world that seemed to have none. Maybe one of those was that when someone dies, the human heart opens itself to strangers. Martin was not a religious man, so it made him all the more nervous to realize that God might be looking him in the eye.

Still, he was pleased to be welcomed into the somewhat familiar home. After asking a few people where to find her, he was finally introduced to Stewart's mother.

Victoria Chinnery had aged gracefully. Her blonde hair was mostly grey now. Her eyes were blue, and her skin was so fair, it almost looked pink in some areas. She greeted Martin with a smile, albeit a sad one.

"How did you know my Stewy?" Victoria asked.

"Uh, I'm a writer for a paper. He was talking to me about his job."

"Ah, yes. The computers. Always with his computers. He loved it there, at CompuCenter."

"CompuCenter?" The name sounded familiar to Martin, but this was the first time he'd heard about it in relation to Stewart. "What do you mean?"

"CompuCenter. You know. Their commercials are on all the time. He didn't work in an actual store, but in one of their offices doing God knows what."

CompuCenter was a retailer of computers and other small electronics, and they also offered computer repair services. Based in Virginia, they had stores all over the Eastern seaboard. It seemed Victoria had no idea who her son really was.

"Anyone else here work with him or go to his office?"

"Oh, no," Victoria said. "He was very shy and kept to himself. I mean, of course there was a chance he had friends at his office, but it's highly unlikely."

Victoria kept the same small smile on her face the whole time. She was polite to a T. But behind that politeness was sadness. Martin noticed how red her eyes and nose were. She was probably all cried out by the time he'd arrived.

They talked a few more minutes. She told him she was a single mother and that Stewart was her only child. The father was out of the picture, and Victoria had doted on her only child. Stewart had gone to college near their home in Portland, and when he earned the job at the NSA—which his mother thought was CompuCenter—no one questioned whether she would move with him. It was all but assumed.

"What kinds of things was Stewart telling you about? I mean, what would make a hot-shot reporter like you come all the way down here from New York?"

He let out a small laugh. "Thanks, ma'am, but I'm no hot shot. And I'm based here in DC."

"Oh. How do you like it?"

"Washington?"

She nodded and hummed a nearly silent "Mmm-hmm." It seemed she was already losing track of what they had been talking about. Martin was grateful; he didn't want to reveal what he and her son were discussing.

He gave a boring answer and took his leave of

Victoria. On his way out, he stopped to talk to the youngest person he could find—a cousin. They exchanged pleasantries and contact information. When Martin asked if the cousin knew where Stewart lived, the man laughed at first, then caught on that Martin wasn't kidding.

"You really don't know?" the cousin asked. "You're in his home, right here. Right now. Momma's boy since the day he was born." Martin laughed, not knowing how else to react. So Stewart had still lived with his mother.

Martin gave the house one last glance before starting his vehicle. Life inside America's bureaucracy could be a sad and lonely one. For once in long while, Martin was grateful to be reporter.

MARTIN ALWAYS FOUND meetings at county coroners' offices strange. But this one was awkward from the moment he walked in.

The building on E Street was nondescript, with no signs on the outside. This was intentional. The macabre nature of the goings-on in the building was not something they wanted to advertise. Martin knew where to find the door, however. Even though he didn't work the local crime beat, all it took was a short walk over to the desk of his friend Augustine Brune. This raised some eyebrows, especially when Martin said he had to stay quiet about what he was working on. He was sure the guys who handled the murder desk would start their own investigation out of plain curiosity, and maybe to try to get a jump on whatever story the politico writer was nursing.

Inside, the building looked like a mix of an office and a hospital. The security, the waiting room—it all seemed very businesslike. But as soon as Martin had the thought, he would see someone in scrubs walk through one of the doors. It was probably one of the few places on earth where the medical and bureaucratic worlds met. *The Motor Vehicles Department of the dead,* Martin thought.

He met resistance as soon as he arrived. The short, round lady with huge glasses who sat at the front desk wouldn't tell him anything. Initially, she greeted him with warmth, but as soon as she found out he was inquiring about Stewart Chinnery, the wall went up. He'd expected that, which was why he had armed himself with a power of attorney letter he'd had Stewart's cousin grab from Victoria. It had taken some time to get it. The family needed time to mourn. But if there was any foul play, like Martin suspected, he would not get a chance at a second autopsy.

Two days after the burial things started to quiet down around Victoria. That's when Martin had decided to go forward with his request. He felt he had to walk on eggshells, but did it anyway. According to the cousin, Mike, Victoria was happy to help anyone who was interested in the life of her only child. Martin had quietly kicked himself when he'd realized he probably could have gotten the power of attorney signed before the body was interred.

After Martin showed the clerk the power of attorney, a supervisor came over. This man was tall and thin, his mustache greyer than the hair on his head. He told Martin it would take several days to get a copy of the records.

And that Martin would need to get the records from another department.

The excuses came one after another. Finally, Martin walked into the hallway and got an idea. He reached out to Augustine Brune once again, this time via telephone.

Augie, as his friends called him, was the regular beat reporter for the paper. He handled everything pertaining to criminal activity in the city. The only exercise Augie got was walking in and out of the office to grab a smoke. Since Martin was more of a political writer, things like dealing with county morgues were not his strong suit. Martin explained to Augie what was happening and the pushback he was getting.

Augie's response stunned him. "Are you sure you want to keep digging into this?" Augie said. "It's probably a big sack of nothing."

"Maybe," Martin conceded, "but I won't know unless I try, right?"

Augie gave a heavy sigh. "Yeah, I guess you're right. You're talking to Scott, right? Silver fox who looks like a beanpole? Pass your phone over to him. I'll chat him up."

Martin handed the manager the phone and let Augie do the rest. He knew he'd owe Augie for this. He wasn't sure if this was worth the social capital he was using, but he had to find out.

The only words that came out of Scott's mouth were "Okay" and "I understand." Never once did he take his stare from Martin's face. He looked as if he wanted to put Martin inside the morgue. Then, without another word, he handed the phone back over.

"Hey, man, thanks for doing that," Martin said

into the phone. "I owe you." But there was no reply. After a moment, he heard the drumming of the dial tone. Augie had already hung up. He looked up to ask Scott what had happened, but all he saw was the back of the man's lab coat as he disappeared toward the back room.

Martin resigned himself to wait.

And wait he did.

Marin was sure Scott wouldn't just leave him here without giving him something. But his doubt grew. Every minute felt like an hour. As soon as he was at his wits' end and about to stand up, Scott came back and handed him a manila envelope.

"How much is this?" Martin asked.

"Don't worry about it," Scott said and walked away again. This time, Martin knew, he wasn't coming back.

It was odd that Scott hadn't asked for payment for an official state document. But he didn't want to press his luck, so he sat down and opened the envelope.

It was just as Stewart's mother had said: death by aneurism. The form was basic. It was signed by a doctor named Dr. Grady Hayer.

Martin looked at both sides of the paper, as if staring at it would change the contents somehow.

But this was Stewart's death certificate, authenticated by this Dr. Hayer.

None of Stewart's friends or family had any idea who would want to hurt him.

It was a dead end.

Chapter 3

H E COULDN'T LET THIS LIE. He wouldn't let this lie. There was something more to it, and Martin had to find out what it was. Stewart Chinnery was dead at thirty-four years old, just before handing over the story of the decade. It very well might have been natural causes, but Martin wasn't happy with that explanation.

He began by doing a little bit of research into Dr. Grady Hayer. What he found was astounding. There were a couple of Dr. Grady Hayers out there, but both outside of DC. There was a Dr. *Greg* Hayer in Washington, but he had retired. And Martin was pretty sure that retired oncologists didn't work at coroners' offices. This mysterious doctor had to fit in to the picture somehow—but how?

Luckily for Martin, help came in an unlikely form: a CIA agent.

Bobby Wriath was a self-described new guy in the CIA world. Originally from Texas, he had been with the Agency for just two years, but in that small time had already worked in Somalia, Greece, and a few other countries he wasn't comfortable disclosing. He tried staying close to home—that home being America—and working his international cases from there. Everything international and outside American borders still had its hands back in the States.

At least, that's what Bobby told Martin. Most of it was a lie, Martin knew, but he also figured there was some truth in there. What was real and what was not was always the question at the back of Martin's mind.

In the journalism world, Bobby would be considered a source. He gave Martin information that he assumed the CIA wanted leaked. Martin wasn't sure how many other people Bobby worked with, though Bobby assured Martin that he hadn't talked to anyone else.

Forever the cynic, Martin spoke to some of his peers at other organizations. Whenever he hinted about Bobby, he was met with blank stares. Some asked Martin to share his source with them. Maybe Bobby was telling the truth. Regardless, whenever Bobby came around, it was out of self-interest. But Martin was fine with that. After all, getting scoops and leaks on national security was in Martin's self-interest as well. He just wasn't sure how much of what he was getting was diamonds or dung.

Bobby had a similar lanky frame to Stewart. The difference was, Bobby's was more filled out. Martin could tell that Bobby exercised. Many of these CIA types had military backgrounds, and he was sure that Bobby was no different.

One day Bobby called and asked to meet as soon possible. They were both at a coffee shop less than two hours later. The pleasantries were quick, as was the shop talk.

"Sorry to hear about your friend," Bobby said.

"Oh yeah?" Martin said. "Who told you about my friend?"

"People," Bobby said. "Just people."

Martin nodded. "Is that why you wanted to meet with me?"

Bobby opened his hands, and with a big smile said, "As much as I love your taste in wrinkled polo shirts, yeah, that's why I called you. I mean, if I know something about your now-dead friend, don't you want to know?"

Martin tried to play it cool. Any new information about Stewart was important, of course, especially coming from an intelligence source. But Martin didn't want to show how badly he wanted this information. It was a dance they had to perform with each other. Bobby would want something from Martin in return, and it was up to Martin to not give too much.

"Sure. What d'ya got?" Martin said.

"What do I got?" It was Bobby's turn to nod, but this time with a pout.

Did I play it too cool? Martin wondered.

Bobby spun his spoon inside his coffee a few times before looking back at Martin. "What I got is that your friend, Stewart, worked for the NSA. He was going to talk to you and now he's dead." He let the spoon drop on the coffee plate with a loud clang. "That's what I got."

Martin knew this, of course. But the fact that someone else had suspicions about what happened was a real development. Martin went with the first question on his mind. "So what do you think?"

"What do I think? I think someone killed your little friend before he could open up his yapper."

They sat there and stared at each other for a long moment. The air seemed to grow still, as if the world had stopped turning. It was simple enough to say something might be fishy, but it was another thing to actually believe it. And they both did.

Martin pressed on, "So who do you think killed him?" He hoped Bobby wouldn't come back with another rhetorical question. Fortunately, he didn't.

"Truth be told, I'm not sure who killed him. But I know who I think might have." Martin stayed silent. "Obviously, my first thought was someone inside the NSA, but who knows. It could have been a million other people."

"Yeah," Martin said, "like who?"

"I dunno. People who would be hurt by his coming forward."

"Who would be hurt besides the NSA if Stewart spoke?" This hadn't occurred to Martin.

"Politicians who greenlighted this. Military folks who made this information actionable. And that's just off the top of my head."

"Oh," was all Martin could say. He felt a little embarrassed that he, a journalist, hadn't come to that conclusion himself. He also wondered if a certain former congressman had made the wrong enemies in the wrong places. Like the NSA.

"Anyway, just thought I'd come by and let you know that someone else knows what you know."

Was that a threat? Martin wasn't sure. For some reason, he didn't think so.

Bobby continued, "I'll try to see what I can find. Probably nothing, but I'll try."

"Who will you ask..." Before he could get the words out of his mouth, Bobby was already waving a hand for him to stop. With one last stare, Bobby grabbed his jacket from the chair and left.

He left Martin to pick up the bill. Martin was sure he'd be paying for this meeting again, sooner or later.

Chapter 4

"WE HAD TO WORK IN COOPERATION," Lieutenant Caleb Hendrick said almost reluctantly.

"Why?" Martin asked.

They were inside the police headquarters in Washington DC. Lieutenant Hendrick was dressed in his normal police uniform, neatly pressed. A man of Hendrick's station didn't work the streets, but he supervised those who did. The only time Hendrick got dirty was when dealing with reporters like himself, Martin thought with a wry inner smile.

Hendrick was probably fortunate not to be on the beat. Although not overweight by any stretch of the imagination, he wasn't svelte, either. He had a pudgy stomach and his arms looked flabby.

His hairline was deeply receding, but he didn't seem to care much. It was still a bit long on the sides, with a few wisps on the top of his head. The only good thing going for his appearance was that he didn't have a single piece of grey hair. His hair was as black as his pupils.

Kendrick pushed his thick glasses up from his wide nose before he responded, "We had to work in cooperation with the feds because of the sensitivity of his occupation."

"Because he was NSA?"

"Because he was NSA," Hendrick parroted. Sensing Martin's next question, he added, "Officially, we have to have our name on everything, but we couldn't actually lead the investigation. That was for the guys in the Bureau."

"So you did take part in the investigation?"

"Of course!" Hendrick seemed almost insulted. "We won't sign off on something unless we've had a good look at it."

"I see." And Martin did see. Since Stewart was an employee of the federal government, the FBI could also handle the investigation. But since Stewart was also technically just another normal citizen, everything had to be laid out as if the local authorities had done everything.

Depending on the situation, those grey areas were dealt with at different levels of cooperation between the federal government and the local police. Sometimes the police did the entire investigation before passing the information to the feds for review; other times the feds did all the work and only handed the police what they wanted them to know. More times than not, it was a hybrid of the two, with both agencies working together. Officially, local police would stamp and seal everything, while unofficially, the same information, plus a bit more, went to the government agencies. Which sort this case was, Martin knew better than to ask.

"And what did you see?"

"What the report says," Hendrick said. He sounded irritated, but then again, he always was. "Our boy died of an aneurysm in his sleep. Nice way to go, if you ask me."

Martin nodded. He didn't care to let the lieutenant know that he understood he was getting nowhere. Just like the morgue, this was a dead end.

FRUSTRATED, Martin was about ready to give up. He called on Bobby Wriath to see if he had come up with anything. Nothing. To add to Martin's worry, his editor wasn't happy that he was chasing a dead lead. He was paid to produce print on paper, not to spin around like a hamster on a wheel of maybes.

What really killed Martin Sherratt was knowing that he had enough to go to print for the public's taste, but not by his standards. Many others had written about the NSA and the spy network created by Americans to be used on Americans. But this was all happenstance and hearsay mixed up with a few educated guesses. The Snowden affair raised the bar of investigative journalism. The stories needed documents, not statements. Especially not ones that were off the record and from a man who was now deceased.

Sure, Martin could print his suspicions and hope to shed a little light on the situation. But that was a bad decision on two fronts: First, because even for his standards, even pre-Snowden, he wouldn't send anything to print that didn't have documents to support it. Second, and more important, it might hurt more than help. Even now, the fact that he could meet with local authorities, and under the condition of anonymity, talk to them about Stewart Chinnery's real employment situation, would go away if he put the media spotlight on the affair. An affair Martin had to remind himself no one would even care about without the proper documentation. It wasn't worth the wrath of the United States government to get out an unverified story that only a handful of people would read and forget about a day later. No, he was on the precipice of something either great or completely inconsequential.

Just when he was about ready to scratch the whole story, something came to mind: how exactly he had gotten this far in the story.

He received one of the greatest writing lessons of his life from one of his college professors. It was a lesson that carried over from writing to life in general.

That professor gave Martin two words that would change his life: *fail more.*

One day in class, this professor went off-syllabus and ranted. He explained how there were more poor writers than good. More bad music than beautiful music. And it went like that for everything. It really didn't matter what or who you knew. It mattered how much you were willing to actually go out there and get it.

Take the Stewart affair. Martin was only where he was because of stubbornness. Rejection after rejection, and he kept on knocking on every door he could. He had signed on to his first major assignment, and he hadn't come all this way just to get shut down. This story would give him the platform to be seen.

So he decided to fail again and get told no again. He called Bobby Wriath, again. No answer, again. Martin stared at his computer screen. There has to be a way! he screamed at himself, looking at the blinking cursor laughing at him. It must've been more than five minutes, but he was brought back to reality by an email. It came in without a subject line. The email address was long and unfamiliar, with a ".no" for Norway at the end. The message was simple:

MEET ME AT ARE USUAL PLACE. I HAVE SOMETHING.

B

Martin grabbed his jacket and left without even logging off his computer. He rushed to the elevator with a huge smile. Sandra, one of his coworkers, gave him a crooked glance in response to his happiness. He would've given anything to tell her what was playing on his mind:

Fail more.

Chapter 5

"YOU REALLY CAN'T LET THIS THING GO, can you?"

"No," Martin said, unable to hide his smile.

"Okay." Bobby nodded and shared Martin's sheepish smile. "Your buddy was mixed up in some stuff with some bad dudes."

"What kind of stuff?"

"Nothing that bad, really." Bobby pouted as he shrugged his shoulders. "Mainly gambling. But he owed some serious people serious money."

"How much?"

"Over six hundred thousand dollars."

Martin let out a low whistle. He asked the question on his mind. "How could he get into that big of a hole? He didn't make that much money."

"No, you're right. Our friend didn't make that kind of money." Bobby paused to smile a thank you to the waitress who'd brought him his coffee. He continued, "But he did make quite a bit gambling. And then lost it, of course."

Martin asked how much Stewart had made. Bobby told him it was over 1.2 million dollars. Martin's eyes were the size of plates. It was as if he had forgotten how to blink. "Who were these guys?"

"British guys who were actually fronts to some Chinese guys."

For the next several minutes, Bobby explained how Stewart gambled with these guys based in the UK. Although they were the face of the operation, the real players were in Hong Kong. Nearly all of the smaller transactions were done locally in England, through bookies, which were legal in the UK. But when it came to higher numbers and better lines, the Brits represented the folks in China. Stewart's surplus of over a million dollars had become a debt of over half a million dollars. And the men in the shadows were tired of waiting.

"So you think these gambling thugs had something to do with Stewart's death?" Martin didn't even give Bobby time to answer. "Sorry, but I just don't buy it."

"I know. That was the first thing on my mind too. But you see, it's an NSA story too."

"How?"

"He may have used some of that fancy software the NSA gave him to find out about the teams he was betting on, and even worse, to find out about the guys he was dealing with. All for his own profit."

"Wow," was all Martin could say. All this time, Stewart was using his access at the NSA to unsuccessfully get an edge on his gambling. Gambling degenerates would always try to cut corners, but rarely did any of them have access to the wealth of knowledge that Stewart Chinnery had. And although Martin had the highest respect for his sources, in particular someone like Stewart, he also had to admit that most of these people were capable of doing bad. After all, becoming an informant, regardless of the justification, was still disloyalty, was it not? And if Stewart was planning on giving up the goods on the NSA, wouldn't it also make sense that he might be up to other things that weren't as up to par as they should have been? The answer to these questions was a big fat yes.

WHAT DID MARTIN HAVE NOW? A lot more, but also a lot less.

He had leads, but they were too far and too spread out. Everything led to England and China, inside dark underworlds he wouldn't have the first idea of how to penetrate.

He knew better than to even consider asking Bobby for help. If there was something nefarious happening to an NSA agent, the government would be leaps and bounds ahead of him on the trail. And the U.S. Government's six trillion dollar economy trumped his modest means.

He did take the obligatory look, but it was high above everything. Just generalizations, really. He found out about some gambling rings in London and some of the Chinese mafias in and around Hong Kong. He wasn't even scratching the surface, and his attention was split in two directions.

Without even knowing it, he started on another project.

Someone who shared Martin's information desk asked if he could help research and fact find on a few things. This made Martin's editor happy, since he was contributing to something that might actually come to fruition.

During a lull in the investigation, however, the

voice in the back of Martin's mind continued to grow. Finally, he had to silence it by going forward with what he wanted to do.

What he wanted was to find out who really killed Stewart. And he was done looking across two continents.

What was he still missing?

First, the doc. The one who signed the death certificate didn't really exist. Martin knew he had to dig into that, but how?

Second, he knew for certain that the government was looking into Stewart's death. If his death were really due to natural causes, it would have been left up to the local police. Why were the local police even working with the FBI? No, there was more to this angle, and he needed to find out.

There was some big piece of information he was missing. The door was closed, but there were still cracks.

He had only one choice, really, and that was to play his hand. He had very little, and he'd risk everything by putting it out there, but what other choice did he have? Continue on a goose chase in two different places he had no access to? Let the story go away? No, he wouldn't have that.

Rather than go straight to press, he decided to

request a Freedom of Information Act request. He wouldn't be putting the story out, but rather letting the powers that be know he was still looking. A story's a story, and if the U.S. government denied the information request, even that would be part of it.

He was going to print eventually. The only question was when.

Chapter 6

TWO DAYS LETTER MARTIN RECEIVED a call he was expecting.

"Bobby?"

"Yup," Bobby replied.

"To what do I owe the pleasure?" Martin was sure Bobby could feel the smile beaming from his face.

"Well, I see you're not gonna drop this. Your little information request set off every alarm bell you could imagine. Every agency in America is probably listening to our conversation."

"I'm sure they're not, but if they are: dear Mr. President, please fix the sidewalk outside my house. It's falling apart."

"Har, har," Bobby said. "You know our spot."

"Yeah?"

"Be there tomorrow. Seven p.m."

"I can't make it tomorrow," Martin said. "I have a deadline, plus dinner with a cousin who'll be in town."

"Tomorrow. Seven p.m." Then the line went dead.

If Bobby was trying to scare him, Martin wasn't about to let it happen. He would go to the meeting, but it wouldn't be under duress.

But then, without warning, the anxiety came. *How did Bobby get my work number?* He rushed out the door with a mind full of what-ifs.

HOW SERIOUS IS THIS? Martin wondered as he walked into his house. He couldn't lie—he was a little nervous. It was more than just the phone call he received at his office. It was the course of action he had taken. He'd known putting in that Freedom of Information Act request would bring the heat, but he'd told himself not to worry. Now that he had done it, he was starting to regret the decision.

He was tired from the day. He hadn't actually done a lot, but the stress had taken its toll. This was the part of the night when he usually put on cable sports and made himself dinner, but he was too tired for that now. Luckily, he had a frozen dinner stashed away for the evening's meal.

The hum of the microwave came to a sudden end Martin's small home was briefly filled with the contraption's incessant beeps.

He brought his steaming plate to the table and began to eat. A minute later he went to grab himself a beer. He needed it after the stressful day.

He sat and took a long drink of his beer as he devoured his food. All he could do was think about what tomorrow's meeting would entail. Would Bobby help or hurt his cause? These spook types were hard to figure out.

There was a knock on the door. *Shit*, he told himself as he wiped his face with a napkin and jumped up to answer the door. There was no need to look through the side window—he knew who it was. His anxiety turned to anger at the interruption. As he opened the door, Martin realized this was probably another scare tactic.

Bobby stepped inside.

"What gives!" Martin said as another man followed Bobby inside. "And who the hell is that?"

"Security," Bobby said as he sniffed around the

house, walking swiftly as if he lived there and had simply misplaced his keys.

"Security for who?"

"For you, to be honest."

That caught Martin a bit off guard, but at the same time it was reassuring. They were here to help.

"Do you have any more of those?" Bobby asked, pointing to the table.

"More of what?"

"Beer."

"Yeah, I'll get you guys some."

"Just one. Our friend here doesn't drink on the job."

The muscle gave a nod. He was taller than both of them, with a neck as wide as his ears. A flat-topped football player type—a regular bodyguard stereotype. Martin knew he was supposed to be comforted by the man's presence, but still a twinge of fear grabbed him.

Martin walked over to the fridge and with his head inside, called out, "And who exactly is our new friend?"

"Don't worry," Bobby said. "There'll be plenty of time for introductions. We have some things to talk about first."

Martin brought out several beers. He was sure this was going to take a while.

"So, what couldn't wait until tomorrow?"

"That little thing you did," Bobby said as he wagged his finger. "It wasn't smart."

"Oh yeah? How so?"

"You know how so." This time it was Bobby who looked upset.

Their visitor was in Martin's periphery, to the right. It looked as if he was eating peanuts or some type of candy.

"I had to do it, man. I had to. This story is going nowhere fast, and I'm going to print with what I have."

"And what do you have?"

"Nothing, really," Martin answered honestly. "But I have enough to get people asking questions. Maybe that's what this story needs. A little more light."

"Okay," Bobby said, although it was anything but. "So what did you find out that made you decide to go to print so fast? Who was it that killed Stewart? The Chinese or the Brits?"

"Neither," Martin said. "It was exactly who I thought all along. Someone here. Someone in the NSA."

"Bullshit."

"Maybe, but it's what I'm going with."

They stared at each other for a few moments. The house filled with an eerie, ear-ringing silence. Bobby began to rub his eyes. "There really is no stopping you from sending this to print, is there?"

"Nope. Sorry."

"Okay." Bobby got up to leave. At least, that's what Martin thought, but soon Bobby was stretching his hands and sitting back down. He was preparing himself for something. For what, Martin wasn't sure.

"Look, I'm done playing games. I'm gonna tell you the truth, Martin. After that, all of this goes away, understand?"

"All what goes away? Look, Bobby, no matter what you tell me, I'm still going to print. You can't..."

"Understand!"

Martin jumped. "Yeah, Bobby. Sheesh, man. I understand."

"Good. Well, just to let you know, I wasn't sending you on a total wild goose chase. Not entirely." Martin stared at him. "Your little friend was a gambling junkie and he did owe some folks across the pond some money."

"Was it as serious as you said?"

"Naw, not really," he admitted, "but it drew you

off the scent. We think, with enough time, Stewart could've paid off his debt. But still, having someone around who could possibly be blackmailed was not a good thing."

"So that's why he was killed?"

"No, no, of course not." Bobby waved his hands animatedly. "If we had to kill every intelligence agent who behaved badly on their free time, we'd have no intelligence community left. No, your friend is dead because of you."

"Because of me?" Martin pointed to his own chest. "You mean because of what he was going to tell me."

"Well, yeah, if you want to get technical about it. We couldn't have another leak. Not this big. He gave us no choice."

"Who is *us*?"

"The United States of America."

Even though he was ready to go to print with the suggestion, at the back of his mind he'd believed it was unlikely. And now that the suspicion was verified, it was a lot to take in. He began to walk to the kitchen, but the muscle stopped him with a hand to the chest. Martin smacked it away. "Get away from me! What the hell is this!" he said, turning to Bobby.

"Please," Bobby said, motioning to the chair. "He

just wants you to have a seat. So we can finish our conversation. Have a seat. Please."

For a few moments Martin stood there with his hands on his hips, shaking his head. He dropped into his seat like a grumpy child.

"We good?" Bobby asked. He didn't wait for a reply. "That's the truth and the whole truth, so help me God."

"Why are you telling me now? You think by telling me this you'll keep me from writing the story I already have?"

"No, no. That's not why I'm telling you. I'm telling you because you left me no choice. You might as well know everything. Who exactly killed him? I know, and I don't know."

"What do mean you know and you don't know?"

"The people who ordered him dead, I mean. I'm not sure exactly who it was, who made the call. Obviously some NSA higher-up, but who, I'm not sure. Probably some snot-nosed Ivy League kid who's never done a hard day's work in his life."

"Then what do you mean you do know who killed him?"

"I know... because I killed him. Broke into his house and waited for him under his bed like a little kid's monster fantasy. Waited an hour, got up, put my hand over his sleeping mouth, and injected him with a needle straight to his liver."

If Bobby was making a joke, Martin didn't appreciate it. "So now what? You're gonna kill me too?"

"Yes. Yes I am."

Martin didn't feel the punch that knocked him out cold.

Chapter 7

MARTIN STARTED TO WAKE UP. It was bright—very bright. He felt cold. He was on a concrete floor. His garage.

His car has been pulled out, and it was just him and his boxes of junk. He felt almost drunk. Had they poisoned him? If so, it wasn't enough to kill him.

Then he realized he was tied up. Inside his mouth was a rag that smelled of oil. Probably one that had been lying around. It was wrapped around his face so tight that the back of his head hurt from the pressure. His wrists were tied behind his back, and his legs and ankles were also bound. He could hardly squirm.

They'd left him there. Why'd they take his car?

He was alone in this brightly lit garage. He knew this part of the story. The bad guys had told him everything before his demise. All that was left to do was escape.

Before he could do that, the door to the garage opened. Bobby and the other man stepped in. They stood in the doorway and talked for a few moments in hushed whispers. After a while, they shook hands and gave each other an embrace. The second man left briefly and returned with a square piece of plywood nearly as tall as the door. He handed it to Bobby. They exchanged a quick nod and the man closed the door behind him, looking at Martin as he did so.

"My real name is Justin Grant," Bobby said. "I'm originally from Montana. My mother's name was Patty and my father's was Justin, just like me.

"I played high school football and I was the star wide receiver at Riverdale High. My sophomore year, I led the entire district in catches made.

"I was married once. Divorced once. I have three sisters, all younger than me. No children, but plenty of nieces and nephews to keep me busy. I joined the Marines. During Operation Desert Storm I killed my first man. I killed others that same night. Later in the war I killed a lot more. I'm not sure how many. Not because I'm some psychopath, but because I was a SAW gunner. Not really sure how many guys I mowed down.

"Now I work for the CIA, and I clean up messes."

Martin wasn't sure why he was being told all of this. Bobby left his line of sight. Martin heard what he thought was the plywood being dragged.

Bobby, or Justin, kicked Martin over so he was lying on his back, struggling with his hands underneath him. Holding the plywood in his hands, Bobby stood over Martin. He gave Martin one last regretful shake of the head and dropped the wood on him. Martin barely had time to turn his head; it smacked him on the side of the face. He was now under a wooden blanket. He could still see, albeit only four inches from the edge of the wood as it hovered off the ground. Bobby's feet moved away and then came back. He was carrying something.

Is that my sledgehammer?

The first blow of the sledgehammer was a total surprise. As pain shot through Martin's chest, he was still in disbelief about what was happening. He wanted to ask what Bobby was doing, but before he could even try, another blow from the hammer came down on the plywood, crushing his chest. Blood began to poor from his mouth and panic seized his body.

He's really going to kill me.

This had to be a lesson. The next blow came crushing down and the bones of his ribcage pierced one of his lungs. He lay there, drowning on his own blood, with tears running down his face.

Mercifully, the next blow missed his chest and went a little high, knocking him out for the second time that night.

He would never wake up.

Chapter 8

THEY HAD NEVER ACTUALLY TAKEN MARTIN'S CAR. They'd merely moved it outside to give them room to finish the job. Now that the job was done, Jason Henry—as Justin Grant/Bobby Wriath was known inside the CIA— drove Martin's car, with Martin's body in the trunk. Jason's partner followed in his truck.

After nearly two hours of driving along a wooded mountainside, they reached their destination.

Jason had scouted it for over a year. It seemed like the perfect spot. There was an area to pull off from the main road and there were no barricades. A little far away, but it was downhill, so it would make pushing the car into place that much easier. It was nearly 3 a.m. and the only traffic was the occasional semi that could be seen coming miles away.

They quickly moved the body into the driver's seat, making sure not to buckle him in. They threw a bevy of empty beer bottles on the car's floor. While Martin lay unconscious and dying, Bobby had injected him with vodka. Toxicology reports can't tell the type of booze, so it didn't matter. His blood would come back with a high BAC.

As they pushed the car with the body inside over the edge of the mountain road, Jason thought how sad it was that all these writer types drank so much. At least that's what he was sure Lieutenant Caleb Hendrick would decide when he finished the investigation.

It didn't matter much to Jason Henry. He had to start preparing for his next mission—one that would take him outside the country.

He was needed off the coast of North Korea.

ALSO BY TONY HERNANDEZ

The Slaughter & Maneuver Books

The Slaughter Trilogy Collects the novel and both short stories

Prologue Collects both short stories

Slaughter & Maneuver The novel that started it all!

The White Can One of two short stories inside the Slaughter & Maneuver Trilogy

Condition of Anonymity One of two short stories inside the Slaughter & Maneuver Trilogy

Novels and Novellas

The Eastern Front 1945 WW2 Historical Fiction set during the dying days of the Eastern Front

The Past Happens Tomorrow Time traveling police procedural

What Doesn't Kill You A globe-spanning Kowalski Thriller set in the final pre-9/11 days

Toulon 1793 Set during Napoleon's first victory and the French Revolution

Driver Heartbroken man thinks he discovers a plot to destroy the world

SHORT STORIES

Tapestry of Lies A Kowalski Thriller short story

ANTHOLOGIES

An Evening In Scottsdale And Other Tales Volume One collection of short stories